CIRCUS

by JACK PRELUTSKY · Pictures by ARNOLD LOBEL

ALADDIN BOOKS
MACMILLAN PUBLISHING COMPANY · NEW YORK

Aladdin Books · Macmillan Publishing Company
866 Third Avenue, New York, NY 10022
Collier Macmillan Canada, Inc.

First Collier Books edition 1978 · First Aladdin Books edition 1989

Printed in the United States of America

10 9 8 7 6 5 4 3 2 1

Library of Congress Cataloging-in-Publication Data

Prelutsky, Jack.
Circus/by Jack Prelutsky; pictures by Arnold Lobel.—1st Aladdin Books ed.   p.   cm.
Summary: Poems and illustrations depict the sights and sounds of the circus.
ISBN 0-689-70806-8   1. Circus—Juvenile poetry. 2. Children's poetry, American. [1. Circus—Poetry. 2. American
poetry.] I. Lobel, Arnold, ill. II. Title.   [PS3566.R36C57 1989]
811'.54—dc 19   88-39841   CIP   AC

For Susan — a great editor, a great friend

Over and over the tumblers tumble
with never a fumble
with never a stumble,
top over bottom and back over top
flop-flippy-floppity-flippity-flop.

They toss and they tumble,
they bounce and they bound
all around and around
hardly touching the ground,
they somersault backwards with never a slip
flip-floppy-flippity-floppity-flip.

Listen to the music, listen to the din
as the marching monkey band comes in
led by a gibbon with a long baton
who waves his musical monkeys on.

Two little capuchins, clever and nimble,
drum on drums and beat on a cymbal.
A big baboon blows a big bassoon,
he's out of rhythm and time and tune.

A chimp named Mike and another named Morgan
pummel on the keys of the circus organ.
A fat woolly monkey plucks on a harp,
a little too flat and a bit too sharp.

A spider monkey tootles a flute.
An ape blows a trumpet with a derby mute.
An orangutan fiddles with charm and grace.
A gorilla scrapes on a double bass.

With brass, percussion, winds and strings
the monkeys ramble through the rings.
Listen to the music, listen to the shout
as the marching monkey band goes out.

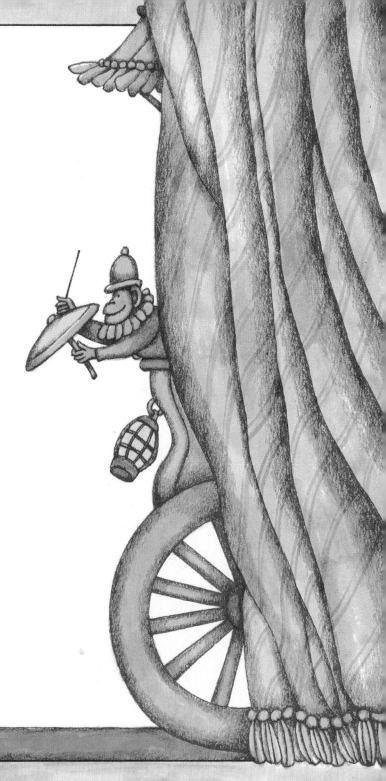

The high-diver climbs to the ladder's top
and gazes down—a long long drop.
She flexes and prepares to go
into the waiting tub below.

With perfect poise, the diver plunges
into the bathtub, stuffed with sponges.
She lands! The sponges slish and slosh.
What a peculiar way to wash.

ENORM

The mightiest strong man on all of the planet
struts about proudly and then with a laugh
he picks up a rock of unbreakable granite
and not even trying he breaks it in half.

The mightiest strong man with muscles like boulders
demonstrates why he deserves his acclaim.
He flexes his arms and he ripples his shoulders
then bends a steel bar so it spells out his name.

The famed sword-swallower, looking bored,
digests a dagger, dirk and sword.
He bows to us, then quickly follows
with epee, foil and saber swallows.

We ooh and ahh, we gape and gawk,
he gobbles down a tomahawk.
And then without a trace of fear
he opens wide and eats a spear.

A dozen arrows piece by piece
precede a cruel Malayan kris.
He's not like us, this swallower,
he's probably much hollower.

The great fire-eater, befitting his name,
lights up a torch and devours the flame.
He follows this torch with another in turn.
They don't seem to scorch him,
they don't seem to burn.

Cinders and embers and fiery coal,
he swallows them, smoldering bowl after bowl.
He gobbles his dinner with evident zeal
then gulps lemonade to extinguish the meal.

Four furry seals, four funny fat seals
Ork! Ork! Ork!
With silly seal stunts for four fish meals
Ork! Ork! Ork!

Four furry seals blowing horns, toot toot
Ork! Ork! Ork!
Flapping their flippers in a seal salute
Ork! Ork! Ork!

Four furry seals bouncing big beach balls
Ork! Ork! Ork!
Croaking clamorous silly seal calls
Ork! Ork! Ork!

Four furry seals striking silly seal poses
Ork! Ork! Ork!
Balancing hoops on their silly seal noses
Ork! Ork! Ork!

Four furry seals, four funny fat seals
Ork! Ork! Ork!
With silly seal stunts for four fish meals
Ork! Ork! Ork!

Sporting and capering high in the breeze,
cavorting about from trapeze to trapeze
is an aerial acrobat, slim as a ribbon,
as daring and free as a tree-swinging gibbon.

He hangs by his fingers, his toes and his knees,
he dangles and dips with astonishing ease,
then springs into space as though racing on wings,
gliding between his precarious swings.

He cheerfully executes perilous plunges,
dangerous dives, unforgettable lunges,
delicate scoops and spectacular swoops,
breathtaking triple flips, hazardous loops.

Then this midair magician with nerves made of steel
somersaults, catches and hangs by one heel.
As the audience roars for the king of trapezes
he takes out his handkerchief, waves it...and sneezes.

Balanced above us, the high wire king
skips with a swivel, a sway and a swing.
He dances, he prances, he leaps through the air,
then hangs by his teeth while he's combing his hair.
He seems not to notice the perilous height
as he stands on his left hand and waves with his right.

My trainer steps into the ring,
then with a quick and graceful spring
I follow him, quite close behind
(my trainer doesn't seem to mind).

He turns and stares into my eyes.
I'm not afraid (I'm twice his size),
but docilely I jump and skip,
obeying when he snaps his whip.

It seems that since he shows no fright
(despite my might, my fearful bite),
I do what comes into his head,
roll over, dance, skip rope, play dead.

Yet though I'm skillful as can be,
I think the crowd cheers him, not me.
I wonder why I always do
exactly as he tells me to.

I tame the very fiercest beast,
the lion, proud and wild,
but I don't fear him in the least,
for me he's meek and mild.

I step into the lion's cage,
he bares his fearsome fangs,
but let him rave and rant and rage,
I feel no fearful pangs.

I boldly stare into his face,
his roar is harsh and loud.
I clasp him in a strong embrace
before the awe-struck crowd.

And when I calmly place my head
between his gaping jaws,
I fear no fear, I dread no dread,
I only hear applause.

The mighty lion wants to please
and so does all he can
because he knows, because he sees
that I'm a fearless man.

Eight big black bears six feet tall,
each one perched on a big rubber ball,
balancing on four legs, balancing on two,
clever tricks you'd never think a bear could ever do.

Eight big black bears playing clarinets,
balancing on barrels, doing pirouettes.
Standing on their heads and hopping over chairs,
eight very talented big black bears.

The wiggling, wriggling, jiggling juggler
joggles and juggles a jangle of things:
hats and platters that clitter and clatter
and canes and chains and rattles and rings.

Blocks and balls of various sizes
ly from the jiggling juggler's hands.
They twist and twirl, they wobble and whirl,
e calmly catches them where he stands.

hen juggling delicate eggs by the dozen
ey'd certainly splatter if ever they'd fall),
h a mystical twist of his wriggling wrist
jiggling juggler catches them all.

wiggling, wriggling, jiggling juggler
les and juggles as nobody can.
nakes all things take magical wings—
ay for the jiggling juggler man!

The famous human cannonball
stands at the cannon's side.
He's very round and very small
and very dignified.

He bows to the east, he bows to the west,
he bows to the north and south,
then proudly puffing up his chest
he steps to the cannon's mouth.

The famous human cannonball
is ready to begin.
His helpers hoist him at his call
and gently stuff him in.
The air is filled with "ahh's" and "oo
preparing for the thrill,
but when his helpers light the fuse
the audience is still.

en in the hushed and darkened hall
 mighty cannon roars,
 famous human cannonball
 oots out and swiftly soars.

Higher and higher the cannonball flies
in a brilliant aerial burst
and catapulting through the skies
he lands in the net—feet first.

Bring on the clowns!
Bring on the clowns!
Clowns wearing knickers
and clowns
wearing gowns.

Tall clowns and short clowns and skinny and fat,
a flat-footed clown with a jumping-jack hat.
A clown walking under a portable shower,
getting all wet just to water a flower.
A barefoot buffoon with balloons on his toes,
a clown with a polka-dot musical nose.
Clowns wearing teapots and clowns sporting plu
a clown with a tail made of brushes and brooms.

HA